LEMONADE with a Twist

by Steven Banks   illustrated by Victoria Miller
based on the teleplay by Jack Thomas

SCHOLASTIC INC.

New York Toronto London Auckland Sydney
Mexico City New Delhi Hong Kong Buenos Aires

D0041835

Butch Hartman (signature)

Based on the TV series *The Fairly OddParents*®
created by Butch Hartman as seen on Nickelodeon®

No part of this publication may be reproduced in whole or in part, or stored in a retrieval system,
or transmitted in any form or by any means, electronic, mechanical, photocopying, recording,
or otherwise, without written permission of the publisher. For information regarding permission,
write to Simon Spotlight, Simon & Schuster Children's Publishing Division,
1230 Avenue of the Americas, New York, NY 10020.

ISBN 0-439-62341-3

Copyright © 2004 by Viacom International Inc. All rights reserved. NICKELODEON,
The Fairly OddParents, and all related titles, logos, and characters are trademarks of
Viacom International Inc. Published by Scholastic Inc., 557 Broadway, New York, NY 10012,
by arrangement with Simon Spotlight, Simon & Schuster Children's Publishing Division.
SCHOLASTIC and associated logos are trademarks and/or registered trademarks of Scholastic Inc.

12 11 10 9 8 7 6 5 4 3   4 5 6 7 8 9/0

Printed in the U.S.A.
First Scholastic printing, March 2004

Crash Nebula on Ice was coming to the Dimmsdale Dimm-a-Dome! "We **must** get tickets!" cried A.J. "No problem," said Timmy calmly.

After his friends left
Timmy called for tickets.
But the show was
completely sold out!

The next day A.J. and Chester
were mad at Timmy.
"Do not worry," said Timmy.
"I can still get tickets."
Timmy took a deep breath
and walked into the boys' bathroom.

"Welcome to Francis's Toilet
of Tickets," Francis said, grunting
as he popped out of the toilet.
Timmy asked him for three tickets to
Crash Nebula on Ice.

But Francis wanted fifteen
hundred dollars!
The boys did not have the money.
"Too bad," Francis said, sneering
as he slid back into the toilet.

Back at home Timmy tried
to wish for tickets. But Cosmo
and Wanda said that it would
be against **Da Rules** to take
the tickets away from someone else.
Timmy had to **earn** the money!

Timmy opened a lemonade stand.
His mother was his first customer.
She took a sip and
immediately spat it out.
"This is horrible!" she cried.

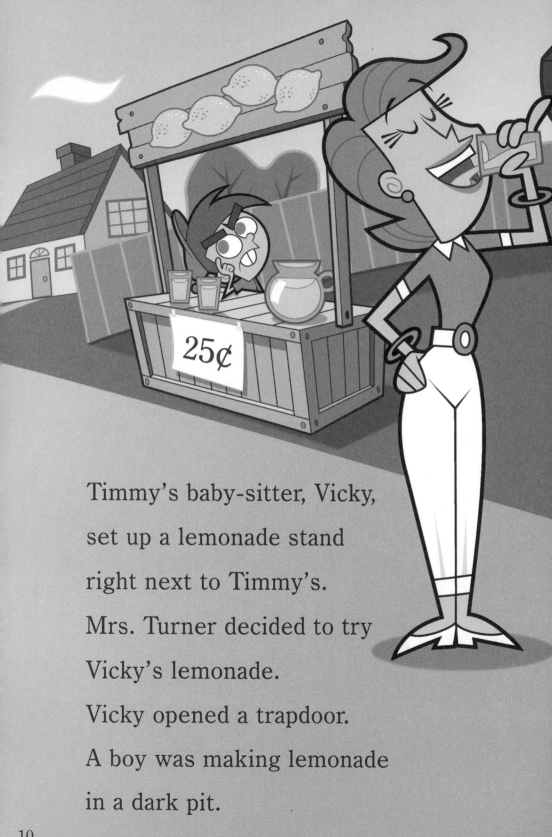

Timmy's baby-sitter, Vicky,
set up a lemonade stand
right next to Timmy's.
Mrs. Turner decided to try
Vicky's lemonade.
Vicky opened a trapdoor.
A boy was making lemonade
in a dark pit.

"One lemonade!" yelled Vicky.
The boy quickly made some
and Timmy's mother took a sip.
"Yummy!" she cried.

Timmy had to make his

lemonade better.

He tried adding cheese,

taco sauce, and peas.

But it was worse than before!

Wanda said Timmy should wish
for sweeter lemonade.
Cosmo then took off his socks and
dipped them in Timmy's glass.
"I said **sweeter**, not sweatier!"
Wanda said with a frown.

Timmy loved the new lemonade.

"I wish I had a whole

pitcher of it!" he yelled.

Before Cosmo and Wanda

could grant Timmy's wish,

a pitcher of lemonade appeared.

A.J. tested the lemonade.

"This is great!" he shouted. "I wish
everybody knew about it!"

Suddenly a news van pulled up
and Chet Ubetcha jumped out.

"Hello, Dimmsdale!" he announced.

"Everybody should try

this lemonade!"

Soon hundreds of people

lined up at the stand.

"At this rate we will **own**

Crash Nebula!" said A.J.

as he counted their money.

Then Timmy saw that they were

almost out of lemonade.

"Man the fort," he instructed.

Timmy ran into the garage.

Cosmo was pedaling on a bike

to make more fairy sweat

for the lemonade.

"Getting . . . tired,"
Cosmo said, moaning.

"Less talkie! More sweatie!"
ordered Timmy.

Outside a little boy gulped
down some lemonade. He wished that
his old dog Speedy was with him.
Then Speedy appeared.
"Wow!" said Timmy.
"When people drink Cosmo's sweat
their wishes are granted!"

Timmy's dad tried the lemonade.
"I wish I did not have to go to work.
I could drink this all day!"

Then a giant lizard gobbled down
Mr. Turner's office building!
"Cool!" said Mr. Turner, grinning.
Suddenly everybody's wishes were
coming true. Mrs. Turner wished
that Mr. Turner was stronger!

Chet Ubetcha wished
that he was
twenty feet tall!

Then the giant lizard stomped toward Timmy's house! **ROAR!**

Timmy raced to his garage.
He found Cosmo slumped over
on the bike.
"Everybody's wishes are
coming true!" yelled Timmy.
"What are we going to do?"

Timmy squeezed the last bit of sweat into a glass. He had enough to make just one more glass of lemonade. **ROAR!** The lizard had arrived!

Timmy grabbed the last glass.

He took a sip as the lizard

was about to attack.

Timmy wished that the lizard

was two inches tall.

POOF! The lizard shrank.

Timmy took another sip and
wished that everything was
back to normal.
But now Timmy had no money.
He could not buy the tickets
to **Crash Nebula on Ice!**

There was still a little lemonade
left in the glass.
He saw the boy
who had worked for Vicky
crawl out of the pit.

"I **must** have something to drink!"
he begged. Timmy gave him
the last bit of lemonade.

"I wish my father were here," said the boy. Suddenly a car pulled up. Out stepped Doug Dimmsdale, owner of the Dimmsdale Dimm-a-Dome. Timmy had found Doug's long-lost son, Dale!

"How can I repay you?"
asked Mr. Dimmsdale.
Timmy wanted three tickets
to **Crash Nebula on Ice.**
Mr. Dimmsdale said it was sold out,
but there was **one** way they
could see the show. . . .

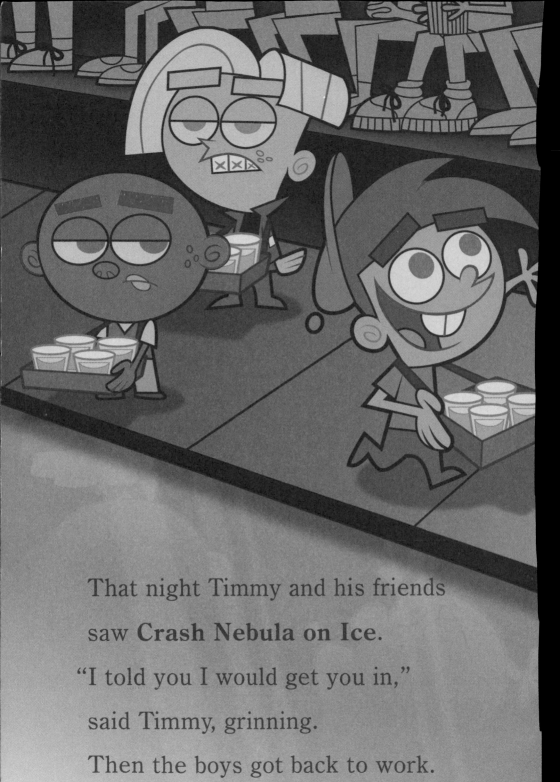

That night Timmy and his friends

saw **Crash Nebula on Ice**.

"I told you I would get you in,"

said Timmy, grinning.

Then the boys got back to work.

"Get your ice-cold lemonade!"